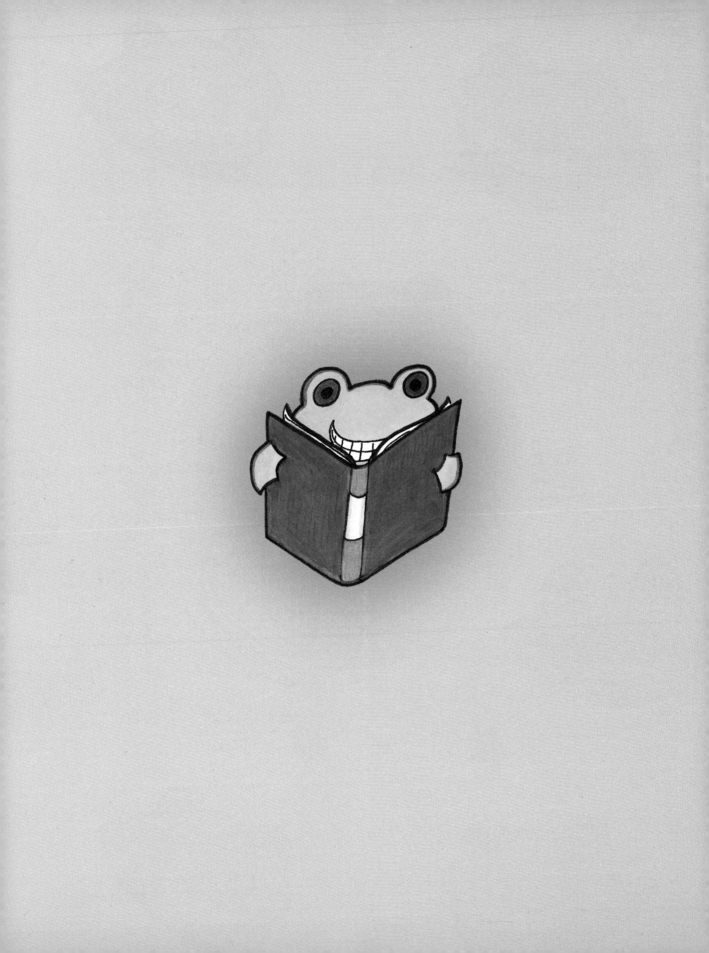

Smile a Lot!

Nancy Carlson

Carolrhoda Books, Inc./Minneapolis

Carolrhoda Books, Inc.
A division of Lerner Publishing Group
241 First Avenue North
Minneapolis, MN 55401 U.S.A.

Website address: www.lernerbooks.com

Library of Congress Cataloging-in-Publication Data

Carlson, Nancy L.
  Smile a lot! / by Nancy Carlson.
      p.   cm.
  Summary: A frog explains how smiling is a great way to get through life's ups and downs.
    ISBN: 0-87614-869-0 (lib. bdg. : alk. paper)
    [1. Frogs—Fiction. 2. Smiles—Fiction. 3. Conduct of life—Fiction.] I. Title.
PZ7.C21665 Sm 2002
[E]—dc21   2001005926

Manufactured in the United States of America
1 2 3 4 5 6 –JR– 07 06 05 04 03 02

To Dede and Kathleen,

Two of the best figure skating coaches ever!

Thank you for twelve years of fun! Keep smiling!

Love from your number one skating mom,

Nancy

Life has all sorts of ups and downs.
That's why you should always

Smile a Lot!

It's much easier than complaining.

When Mom makes oatmeal with prunes for breakfast . . .

Smile a lot! And ask if you can help her
make chocolate chip pancakes tomorrow.

Then figure out what to do with your oatmeal.

Smile a Lot!

It helps you make friends.

If you're the new kid in school,
don't sit in a corner frowning.

Smile a lot! You won't be alone for long!

Smile a Lot!

It confuses the tough guys.

When the tough guys are hogging the swings . . .

Play on the monkey bars and smile a lot! The tough guys
will think you're having more fun than they are.

Soon you'll have the swings to yourself!

Smile a Lot!

It gets you through the hard times.

When you only get three words right
on your spelling test . . .

Just smile a lot and no one will know
you only got three words right.

And when you show the test to your mom and dad,
smile a lot and tell them you'll do better next time.

Then study hard and next time,
you might get a perfect score!

Smile a Lot!

It gives you lots of courage.

When you have to go to the dentist for a checkup,
smile a lot!

You'll discover the dentist is really not so bad.

You might even get a prize or two for bravery!

Smile a Lot!

It helps you reach your goals.

When you have to run a whole mile at soccer practice,
smile a lot!

Smiling takes a lot less energy than moaning and groaning.
Then you can run so fast that . . .

Your coach just might start you at forward
in the next game!

When nighttime comes

And you're starting to fall asleep . . .

Smile a lot because

You've had a pretty good day!